To Ffion
Don't stop dreaming!

A.H Proctor is a successful businesswoman, wife and mother who has unashamedly lived in a fantasy world for most of her life. Captivated from childhood by fairy stories and the world of the Brothers Grimm, her fertile imagination was held in check until she took her own young children to the beautiful and mystical Scottish Isle of Arran.

When, one day, they asked her to tell them a story of witches and goblins, the floodgates opened.

Inevitably, Angela could not resist taking it a stage further and she began to write.

The *Thumble Tumble* stories, set on mysterious Arran, were born.

Angela has discovered that she has not only released her inner child – but found a way to escape the pressures of her high-powered 'day job' as an executive with a financial services company.

Thumble Tumble and the Ollpheist is the first instalment in a series of eight.

Thumble Tumble
And The Ollpheist

A.H. PROCTOR

Thumble Tumble
And The Ollpheist

Vanguard Press

A CIP catalogue record for this title is
available from the British Library.

ISBN: 978 178465 060 5

*Vanguard Press is an imprint of
Pegasus Elliot Mackenzie Publishers Ltd.*
www.pegasuspublishers.com

First Published in 2015

**Vanguard Press
Sheraton House Castle Park
Cambridge England**

Printed & Bound in Great Britain

For Skye and Kyle, my little book worms and for Jessie, who never stopped believing

Chapter 1

The Broken Coven

A long, long time ago there existed a coven of witches that gathered together the most powerful witches from all of the islands on earth. The coven gathering brought together witches from as far north as Iceland, and the beautiful island of Heimaey, to the tropical islands of Thailand and the glorious Isle of Arran just off the coast of Scotland.

Within the coven lay the balance of good and evil on earth, as the coven was made up of good witches or white witches as they are often known and dark witches, mainly 'Night Witches', the most evil and powerful of all dark witches.

This balance had prevailed throughout the centuries until an extremely powerful Night Witch called Mogdred decided she wanted to rule over the coven and so a struggle between good and evil began. Mogdred turned witch against witch and used her powers to destroy any creature that stood in her way.

Over the years, Mogdred and her followers destroyed hundreds of white witches and as she did dark forces began to appear on earth. As when the coven was broken, so too was the equilibrium between good and evil.

As Mogdreds' powers grew, the darkness spread, engulfing everything that lay before it and if not stopped, soon she would cover the whole world in a blanket of evil and good would be gone forever.

This could not be allowed, and so the elders called a meeting of the witch council and it was agreed by all that Mogdred had to be stopped. The elders knew that without good, evil could not exist either. So everything on earth, good or evil, would be destroyed.

The council selected three sisters, Isla, Bessie and Lizzie from the Isle of Arran to stand against Mogdred and put an end to her tyranny.

When Mogdred arrived on the Isle of Arran the three sisters were waiting for her. One sister had the gift of spell binder. She could cast any spell from the book of enchantment and had created many spells of her own. The second sister was an alchemist who could make all manner of magical potions and the third, the youngest sister, Lizzie, had a powerful amulet that had been given to her by their mother.

An amulet is usually a piece of jewellery, but in fact can be anything, and Lizzie's was a little white handkerchief she wore tied around her wrist. The amulet itself is only a physical object holding the witch's power; it is not the source of the power as this comes from within the witch herself, from her very soul and can only be passed from mother to daughter on death. Lizzie had been by her mother's bedside when she died. She was crying into a little handkerchief when her mother's powers transferred from the silver locket around her neck into the handkerchief clutched tightly in Lizzie's hands.

Lizzie's mother had been a protector of the coven and as such she had been given great powers from the elders to help her defend the coven against all enemies. The powers bestowed upon a protector come from all witches, so a protector has the same powers as every witch on earth. The force of these powers together is so strong that they cannot be held within a witch's body, so they are held within an amulet that can only be controlled by its owner.

Isla was standing on the road at the edge of the Light and Dark forest when she felt the night air turn icy cold, and the sky was covered in a huge black cloud. The Night Witches had arrived. Night Witches are loathsome creatures, with black skin, hair, teeth and nails, which makes them practically invisible at night. They usually keep their eyes closed as they can see through their thin black eyelids so the only way to detect them is from their foul breath which smells like the bottom of a sewer. If they do open their eyes, they can be seen right away as their eyes are bright white with no pupils in the centre, making even the slightest glimmer of light blinding to them. This is one of the reasons they only ever attack under the cover of darkness.

Mogdred had her two daughters with her, Sloth and Gretch, who were both extremely overweight and very lazy. Neither had wanted to fly all the way to Arran and they were still moaning about how long it was since they had last eaten when they walked straight into Lizzie. Before they could even lift a finger Lizzie flicked her wrist and they both went flying through the air. Sloth landed with a thud so hard that there was an imprint of her huge bottom on the ground and Gretch hit a tree with such force that it snapped in two and the top half of the tree landed right on her head.

Sloth sat up and pointed her long black finger towards Lizzie, but it was too late. Lizzie was already twirling her finger around in a circle and smiling at Sloth. Next thing she knew Sloth was spinning around and around up in the air and a rope was wrapping itself around her feet, then around her hands, and finally it wrapped around her face like a gag then she dropped back onto the ground with another huge thud. Lizzie turned her attention to Gretch who had climbed out from under the tree and was casting a death curse towards her. Lizzie ducked as the spell shot out of Gretch's long black finger and went right over the top of Lizzie's head like a thunder bolt.

Mogdred, however, did not miss. She was standing right behind Lizzie when she cast her deadly spell and the bolt hit Lizzie in the middle of her back. She fell to her knees just as Isla and Bessie appeared from the dark clouds above on their brooms.

"No!" screamed Isla as she swooped down towards Mogdred. She was carrying a small pink vase that she threw straight at Mogdred's head. The vase hit Mogdred right between the eyes and shattered into tiny pieces allowing the thick brown liquid inside to pour over Morgdred's face. At exactly the same time Bessie started to cast a powerful spell to turn night into day. As she chanted her spell the black clouds parted, allowing shards of light to penetrate the darkness and the sun started to come up on the horizon. Within seconds, bright sunlight covered the whole island. Mogdred started howling in pain as the skin-thinning potion that Isla had thrown on her face began to erode the thin layer of skin covering her eyes. The pain from the blinding light was excruciating, as the skin disappeared completely exposing her vulnerable white eyes to the full force of the sun.

Bessie and Isla flew down to Lizzie's side. She was now lying on the ground, crouched up like a baby with the glass from the broken vase surrounding her like a bed of rose petals. She could barely breathe so every word she spoke was making her weaker.

"Do not despair, my sisters, good has prevailed." She forced the words up from her failing lungs.

Then, with almost no sound at all she whispered, "But I do fear this battle is not over yet."

A single tear rolled down her cheek and landed on a piece of broken glass. Then a little white light hovered up from the handkerchief on her wrist and wrapped itself around the tear drop. Lizzie was dead. The sisters knew what they must do. Bessie cast a forging spell that turned the piece of glass into a small ring, which she placed carefully into her pocket.

She got up and started to walk towards the Night Witches. Gretch was holding Mogdred under her arms and trying to carry her through the trees with her feet dragging along the forest floor. They were heading into the dark part of the forest towards the swamps where she knew they could escape. Bessie used all of her might to cast a pausing spell. She pushed her hand straight up to the sky, pointed her finger towards the heavens and said Stillamonentum. A pausing spell stops time for a few seconds. It's one of the most difficult spells to conjure with only a few witches in the whole world able to do it. As soon as she had uttered the spell, the leaves falling from the trees froze, drifting in mid-air, and Gretch's size eleven feet were floating three inches off the ground as time stood still. The spell took every drop of Bessie's energy. Her arm flopped down to her side and her head dropped forward then tilted to one side. She was so drained all she could do was watch, as Sloth pulled the statue like bodies of Mogdred and Gretch onto her broom and then flew off deep into the forest. The Night Witches were gone... for now.

Chapter 2

The Good Witches

"Toe of toad, slime of snail, drop them in and stir it well.

"Sprig of heather, buzzards feather, add the lot then have a smell.

"Not quite right, add pinch of night, snot of newt and an old black boot."

"Ah, perfect," said Auntie Isla.

Auntie Isla was making her famous 'Scoffalicious Chocolate'. She was the oldest witch on Arran. She was one hundred and fifty-nine years old with long silver curly hair, grey eyes and a thin pointy face. The strange thing about witches is that although they look older when they age, they don't change much physically. A witch can live up to two hundred years old and they'll still be as fit as a human aged fifty! Auntie Isla used to be very tall as a young witch, almost six feet, but had shrunk over the years and was now barely five feet. She wore a long purple dress that she tripped over when she walked as she never got it taken up over the years and so it was now a foot too long! She also wore a small green pointed hat which glistened so much it looked as though it was covered in green glitter. In fact, it was just green dust from making all of her unusual potions.

Auntie Isla's Scoffalicious Chocolate is magic chocolate that always tastes like the favourite food of the person eating it. If you love raspberry ice cream topped with candyfloss then the chocolate tastes just like raspberry ice cream and candyfloss. Even if you like something really gross like slugs wrapped in lettuce leaves, then that's what flavour the chocolate will be... yuck!

Auntie Isla was busy making a giant batch of Scoffalicious Chocolate for King Rohan, the king of the Deer Folk. It was the Great Games today and the King had ordered ten gallons of Scoffalicious Chocolate to serve along with honey wine and berries for after the games. Auntie Isla had a huge cauldron filled to the brim with Scoffalcious Chocolate on the stove in the centre of the kitchen, with several other batches already prepared and in pots ready to go.

The kitchen appeared to be really small but it had loads of things in it. There was a stove in the centre of the room, two large fridges – one on either wall – along with various cupboards, sinks and chopping boards dotted around the room. There was also a small purple trampoline in the corner under the window and a tight rope that stretched from one wall to the other right above the stove. It was a very, very unusual kitchen indeed.

Blue smoke started billowing up the chimney from the chocolate that was boiling on the stove. The smoke wafted up the chimney and out into the cold morning air. There was often strange coloured smoke or sparks coming out of Auntie Isla's chimney. If it wasn't from Auntie Isla's strange cooking it would be from one of Auntie Bessie's wacky spells.

The smoke looked like big long blue shoe laces which twisted and spiralled around the kitchen. The smoke passed through the open kitchen door and up the staircase to the little bedroom at the top of the stairs. First the blue shoelaces wrapped themselves around the silver door knob that was shaped like a star fish then it seeped in through the tiny crack which ran all the way around the door as it didn't quite close properly. The blue smoke shoelaces then drifted up each one of Thumble Tumble's nostrils waking her up from the most amazing dream. She was dreaming she was eating giant chocolate covered strawberries when she woke up. Either that, or the chocolate aroma had made her dream about the chocolate strawberries and then she woke up!

Thumble Tumble was a good witch who lived in a little white cottage with her Auntie Isla and her Auntie Bessie on the Isle of Arran. She was eight years old and had lived with her aunties for as long as she could remember. Thumble Tumble had shoulder length blonde curly hair, light blue eyes and pale white skin. She was very small for her age, so small in fact that her hat was almost as tall as she was. Like all witches hats, her hat was tall and pointed but rather than being black or grey it was bright blue and in the winter she would pop a pom pom on the point and go sledging on her broom.

Thumble Tumble's favourite colour was pink and she would always have something pink on, even if it was just her little pink ring. She had had the ring ever since she was a baby and it was the only thing she possessed from her parents so it was very precious to her. It now only fitted onto her pinky finger. The ring was completely made of glass with a tiny glass tear drop as the centre piece.

The smell of the Scoffalicious Chocolate was now overwhelming. Thumble Tumble couldn't stay in bed a moment longer. She quickly jumped out of bed and rushed downstairs to the kitchen almost standing on poor Flopsy as she ran out of the bedroom door. Flopsy was Thumble Tumble's cat and as you would expect from a girl who loves pink, Flopsy's fur was bright pink and really soft and fluffy. Other than that, Flospy was just like any other cat: she liked milk, sleep and being stroked and that was about that.

When Thumble Tumble burst through the kitchen door Auntie Isla was pouring the last batch of Scoffalicious Chocolate into pots and placing them by the door.

"Am I in time?" Thumble Tumble said anxiously.

"Of course you are," said Auntie Isla and handed Thumble Tumble a big wooden spoon covered in Scoffalicious Chocolate.

When she had licked every last drop of chocolate off of the spoon Thumble Tumble finally said good morning to Auntie Bessie who was now standing over the stove trying to cast a spell to get the cauldron to clean itself.

"Abrika, hocus and twiddle e dee…"

Nothing was happening.

Auntie Bessie was brilliant at casting spells, but she was also a bit wacky and sometimes this would carry into her spells. Like the time when she was trying to cast a freezing spell on a Tree Troll and instead of freezing the Tree Troll, she cast a spell that put a sheet of ice over the whole of Arran and it was freezing for a week!

"Alacazam, alacazum, make the dirt on this cauldron disappear with the touch of my thumb."

She touched the cauldron with her thumb and suddenly there was a puff of green smoke. Then plop, plop, two legs popped out of the bottom of the cauldron. The legs were really skinny, like two twigs with huge feet at the bottom. They were wearing stripy red and white socks and running shoes and then, whoosh the cauldron got up and ran straight out of the front door.

This was not what Auntie Bessie had in mind, but the dirt had at least disappeared.

"I'll head out later and find the cauldron. Hopefully before anyone sees it," she said with a sigh.

Auntie Bessie had been very beautiful in her youth and although older now – one hundred and twenty-two – you could still see the beauty that lay behind her wrinkles. She had short, spiky jet-black hair, dark brown eyes and rosy lips. Auntie Bessie wore a rainbow coloured dress, a patchwork of different colours and textures made up of cloth, leaves, fur and wool that came all the way down to her toes. She didn't wear any shoes and instead of having a cat as her companion, Auntie Bessie had a little bat called Podi.

Podi was a stinky little bat who did not like washing, flying or walking and so lived under Auntie Bessie's hat so that he could travel wherever she did without ever having to stretch his wings – which he also didn't like doing.

"Who is all this Scoffalicious Chocolate for?" asked Thumble Tumble.

"It's for King Rohan," said Auntie Isla. "It's part of the feast for after the Great Games today."

King Rohan was the King of the Deer Folk. Half human, half deer the Deer Folk lived in the grounds of Lochranza Castle. Deer Folk are very powerful creatures with human torsos and the legs and antlers of a deer. They are toned and muscular and have the strength of ten human men when they are fully grown.

Thumble Tumble had met King Rohan a long time ago when she was very little. She couldn't remember much about the time she had met him, her memory was very foggy. She thought it might have been at night as it was dark and she remembered a big circle of black witches flying on their brooms around her head. There were men with what she thought were horse legs and horns, firing silver arrows from huge bows at the black witches. At first she thought they were some sort of devils with horns but later she found out it was antlers and that the strange looking men were in fact Deer Folk.

Thumble Tumble had heard all about the Great Games from Auntie Isla and Auntie Bessie. They sounded awesome and she was desperate to see them for herself. Every year she had been told that it was dangerous at the games and that she was too little to go and she knew that this would be the same answer this year if she asked to go. Instead, she thought of a plan.

"Can I help you deliver the Scoffalicious Chocolate to the castle?" she innocently asked Auntie Isla.

Auntie Isla knew that Thumble Tumble was offering to deliver the chocolate in the hope that she would be able to sneak in and see the games, but she also knew that the games wouldn't start for hours. What Thumble Tumble didn't know was that the first event didn't kick off until the sun was setting and so there was no chance of sneaking in this early in the morning.

"Of course you can deliver the chocolate, just remember to be home before dark," said Auntie Isla and she kissed Thumble Tumble on the forehead.

Yes, thought Thumble Tumble. *The plan has worked.* She raced back upstairs to her bedroom which was in the eaves of the little white cottage on Hospital Road. Hospital Road was a quiet road with a peaceful feeling about it as very few cars, or people for that matter, ever travelled along the road. There were only five cottages and at the bottom of the road was a little stretch of stoney beach from which you could see the beautiful Holy Isle across the sea. At the top of the road there was a cemetery with lots of old headstones with the names of humans who had died a long time ago. The cemetery was supposedly haunted at night time, but Thumble Tumble had never gone in at night to find out if this was true or not.

The little white cottage had two chimneys from which there was always some bright coloured smoke or sparks shooting into the sky. This was a bit strange as there was only one fire inside the cottage which was under the stove in the kitchen and so no one could ever work out where the other chimney smoke was coming from.

At the front of the cottage, there was a black wooden door and the door had a ship's porthole right in the middle of it. You couldn't see into the cottage through the porthole from the outside but from the inside it acted like a big magnifying glass making the face of anyone knocking on the door look gigantic. Their eye would look as though it was the full size of the porthole if they tried to peer in. Thumble Tumble found this quite scary sometimes, especially if a little housefly was hovering over the porthole, as from inside the cottage it looked like a monster fly trying to get inside to gobble her up. Although the door was made of wood if you licked it, it tasted like liquorice and Thumble Tumble couldn't resist having a lick at the door every time she came in.

The cottage had two small square dormer windows that popped out of the slanting roof. One window looked out from Thumble Tumble's bedroom and the other looked out from Auntie Bessie's room. Both rooms looked tiny from outside, and they were. The ceiling slanted downward from the centre of each of the rooms to the floor at the edge of the rooms. Thumble Tumble was small enough that she could just about stand up in her room without banging her head. But Auntie Bessie was forever banging her hat off of the slanting ceiling in her room which would of course wake up poor Podi from his permanent state of sleep.

"Ouch!" you would hear Podi squeal out from under Auntie Bessie's hat first thing in the morning when Auntie Bessie would wake up and forget to duck down as she stepped out of bed. This acted like an alarm clock for Thumble Tumble and Auntie Isla as Auntie Bessie woke up every morning at seven a.m. sharp with a loud "Ouch!" from Podi.

Chapter 3

Lochs, Castles and Rumours

Thumble Tumble got dressed into a pink dress with a big silver star on the front, stripy green and yellow tights, pink converse trainers and her bright blue hat which she pulled down to just above her eyebrows. It was February and there was snow on the ground outside so Thumble Tumble had attached a big pink woolly pom-pom to the point of her hat. She went back downstairs and got her broom from the broom cupboard under the stairs along with her red wool cloak, then headed into the kitchen and started loading the pots of Scoffalicious Chocolate into the little basket attached to the back of her broom. The basket was only the size of a small basket you would attach to the front of a bicycle but it was a magic basket and could carry the equivalent of twenty shopping bags. Into the basket she loaded all twelve pots of Scoffalicious

Chocolate, a strawberry jam sandwich, bottle of water, two big juicy green apples and an old picnic blanket.

"I'm off!" she shouted and she hopped onto her broom.

"Remember to be back before dark," Auntie Isla said and then, before she could say another word, Thumble Tumble had disappeared through the porthole in the front door. The porthole was a magical porthole that would open as soon as it detected a white witch on a broom either outside or inside the cottage. The glass in the porthole evaporated into thin air and the porthole itself would stretch out to the full size of the door in an instant. As soon as the white witch entered or left the cottage the porthole would shrink back to its normal size and the glass would reappear closing the porthole shut tight. If the porthole detected a dark witch, it would automatically put a protective magical cloak over the cottage and send a red and gold shot up into the sky that would blast like a firework right above the cottage showering red and gold sparks out across the sky, as a warning sign that could be seen for miles around.

Thumble Tumble shot out into the cold winter air and then soared high into the sky where she couldn't be seen by any humans below. The code of witches, good and bad is that they never let humans see them unless it is absolutely necessary. For good witches this is usually when they are saving a human from some fiendish creature trying to scoff them. And for bad witches, well, they usually are the fiendish creature.

Just below Thumble Tumble's broom was a little white cloud. This was always below her broom during the day so that if a human did happen to look up high into the sky all they would see was a little cloud and not a witch with a big blue hat flying around on a broom!

She flew north towards Lochranza Castle, cutting through the cold air on her broom, looking down at the snow-covered cottages below. The road to Lochranza was a straight road that followed the shoreline all the way to the village of Sannox then cut inland through the Giant Hills to Lochranza. She followed the road below until she came to the Pony Woods when she decided to take a little detour off the road so that she could skim through the trees in the woods. She loved flying through the woods in the winter. She would whizz in and out of the leafless trees watching the sparkling swirl of ice particles fall to the ground as she sped through the bare branches on her broom. She flew back out of the woods and followed the road below again all the way to Lochranza Castle.

The castle looked like an old ruin from outside. It had four grey turrets, and all but one was crumbling away from decades of wind and rain beating against them. A tall wall connected each of the turrets making a perfect square around the internal courtyard and the walls like the turrets were falling away in parts from the weather erosion over the years. There was a huge black wrought iron gate in the centre of the front two turrets which had sharp spikes all the way along the top and bottom of the gate. The gate looked as though it was in perfect condition. No bits missing or falling apart from erosion. In fact, it looked like a brand new gate which had been designed to look like it was about five hundred years old.

Although the castle looked like it was falling apart and would be easy to get into, it was quite the opposite. There was no way into or out of the castle other than through the huge iron gates at the front. The castle walls were very high. Even at the parts where it was eroding away it was still at least the height of two double decker buses stacked on top of one another, so no one could just climb in.

The castle was also protected from intruders trying to fly in from the skies above by the Deer Folk lying in wait in the turrets with their huge wooden bows, which could shoot solid silver arrows hundreds of feet into the air.

The last of the castle's defences was really quite ingenious and mainly just to keep humans away. It was put there by a wizard who took refuge in the castle one Halloween after being chased there by an angry mob of humans who thought he was a witch, which technically he was – just a male witch. He cast a spell that put a border of hypnotic gas all the way around the castle. The gas was invisible and had no smell so that humans don't know they are breathing it in. When they take a breath close to the perimeter of the castle, the hypnotic effects of the gas plays tricks with their mind making them believe all they can see is an old castle ruin. This is the reason why humans very rarely ever see any Deer Folk and if they do they just think they have seen a deer and that their eyes are playing tricks on them!

The castle sits on the banks of the Domhain Loch. The loch is as black as night. When you look into the water all you see is your own reflection looking back at you from the surface as if you are looking at a photograph of yourself that's been printed onto shiny black glass. The loch is impenetrable by the naked eye and so black that no one dares put their hand into the water, just in case.

There are stories about the loch that stretch back for centuries. Many tell of the hideous four headed sea creature the Ollpheist, which is supposed to live at the bottom of the loch five hundred miles below the surface. No one really knows how deep the loch actually is and anyone who has ever gone in to find out has never returned.

Rumour has it that the Ollpheist has four long necks with a different head attached to each. One head has twenty eyes and pincers like a giant spider, another has three black horns and razor sharp teeth. The third is the head of Devil Ogre with fangs that carry poisonous venom, and the fourth looks like a cyclops with one eye right in the centre of its huge forehead.

Chapter 4

Rhino Dust

When she arrived, Thumble Tumble set her broom down beside the loch and got off. She carefully laid her broom flat on the ground then unloaded the twelve pots of Scoffalicious Chocolate and stacked them up beside the iron gates at the front of the castle. She gently ran her fingers along the bars of the iron gates tapping each one as she did so and waited for an answer. This is, of course, the polite way to knock on the door of an enchanted castle. There was no answer. She ran her fingers across the gates again, this time tapping each bar with her index finger, a little harder. The gates didn't budge and from the outside the castle looked completely deserted, but then it would, to anyone affected by the hypnotic gas. Thumble Tumble thought she must be too early. It was only nine o'clock in the morning after all and Deer Folk are not known as early risers.

Thumble Tumble decided to wait for the Deer Folk to wake up rather than just leaving the chocolate outside the gates. If she did that she'd definitely not manage to sneak into the games. So, she got the old picnic blanket out of her basket and laid it out on the ground beside the loch. The blanket was covered in dust and when Thumble Tumble laid it out there was a cough and a splutter. This didn't come from her. It was the blanket coughing and spluttering from its own dust. She picked it up and gave it a good shake then laid it back down on the ground. As soon as she had flattened it out the blanket started crumpling up. Then it began twitching and popping up off the ground by a few inches at first, then finally the whole blanket lifted up into the air, shook itself frantically, and fell back down onto the ground. It was now clear of dust and perfectly flat and smooth with a little green plastic table and chair sitting right in the middle of the blanket. On the table was a white plate and matching cup and a set of shiny cutlery. There was also a book sitting on the table with the title HOMEWORK in capital letters right across the front cover.

Thumble Tumble plonked herself into the chair and picked up the book. The book opened by itself and announced in a piercing high-pitched voice, "Today's lesson is arithmetic and how we use numbers in every day spells."

The book then launched into a series of spells using numbers. The first was the levitating spell where you have to know the exact weight of the object you are lifting with the spell otherwise you will either not be able to lift the object as it will be too heavy, or if you under estimate the weight of the object you could send it all the way out to space. This had in fact been done in the past by none other than Auntie Bessie. As a young student, Auntie Bessie had used the levitating spell on a pair of shoes – her shoes – and she sent them so high into the sky that they ended up in space orbiting the earth for the past hundred years.

After three hours of lessons and no response at the castle gates Thumble Tumble decided it was time for lunch. She went back into the basket attached to her broom and got out her strawberry jam sandwiches, water and apples. She was putting them down on the table when one of the apples dropped onto the ground and rolled right into the loch. *Oh rubbish*, thought Thumble Tumble. *I'll never get that back.* Then, from out of the loch, the apple flew through the air and landed right on top of the pink, woolly, pom-pom on her hat.

Thumble Tumble wasn't sure what to do as she had heard the stories of the terrible sea creature that lived at the bottom of the loch. She was still deliberating whether to make a run for it on foot or take flight on her broom when the apple fell off her hat and rolled straight back into the loch.

Two seconds later, it came hurtling back out and this time hit her right on the nose. Thumble Tumble acted instinctively as she picked up the apple and threw it with all her might back into the loch. *No one smashes me on the nose with an apple and gets away with it*, she thought.

Then she remembered about the Ollpheist and gulped. But instead of a hideous four headed monster coming out of the loch, the apple appeared again, this time landing on the plate on the little green table. Thumble Tumble was so engrossed with the flying apple that she hadn't noticed she had company in the form of a nineteen foot giant.

Rhino was a Spike Back giant. Spike Back giants live in the hills that surround Lochranza Castle. They rarely come down from the hills as they don't like being shot at with silver arrows by the Deer

Folk that live in the castle and like everyone else they had heard the rumours of the Ollpheist that lived at the bottom of Domhain Loch and didn't fancy ending up as the sea monster's dinner!

As their name suggests, Spike Back giants have spikes that run all the way down their backs from their neck to the base of their spine. The spikes look a bit like rhinoceros horns, hence the nickname Rhino. They are ugly creatures with green skin that also resembles a rhinoceros's skin with its thick wrinkly texture. They have black beady eyes and lips that roll inside their mouth. This is because they don't have any front teeth, just big molars at the back of their mouth so they usually sook their victims like a lollipop for a while before popping them in their mouths and chewing them up with their back teeth.

Rhino hadn't planned to come down to the castle this day. He had been minding his own business asleep under a tree, high up in the hills when he was rudely awoken with a huge dollop of dust that landed right on his face and nearly choked him. It got right up his nose and in his eyes making them itchy and red. He got up to wipe the dust out of his eyes but this made him start to sneeze. He sneezed so much that he lost his balance, fell down and basically rolled all the way down the hill only stopping when he banged into the castle walls. This was rather lucky as a few feet more and he'd have been in the loch.

Witches are not high up on the list of favourite food for a Spike Back giant. They are usually fairly small and this witch was particularly small. Spike Back giants don't have any taste buds either, so all they really care about is the size of a meal rather than its flavour. Nonetheless, he was pretty hungry and a small snack between meals would do him no harm at all, or so he thought.

Thumble Tumble picked up the apple from her plate, spun round and lobbed it straight at Rhino's left eye which was already sore and swollen from the dust. She had heard Rhino tip toeing up behind her. At nineteen feet tall and weighing the same as a truck, it was pretty difficult to sneak up on anyone. Rhino let out a scream that echoed for miles through the hills above, then he lunged forward to grab Thumble Tumble. Thankfully, he was still a bit dizzy from rolling down the hill and just grabbed a handful of air instead. She looked around for her broom but it was still lying on the ground beside the castle gates, right behind Rhino.

There was nowhere for her to go and Rhino knew it. "Decisions, decisions, my dear," he mumbled through the gap in his lips. "Would you like to be eaten by me or by the Ollpheist?" He paused for a second then mumbled, "Probably better the devil you know." Thumble Tumble started to walk backwards towards the loch. She didn't know how far she could go before ending up in the water, but she certainly wasn't just going to walk straight into Rhino's lips.

Before she realised what she had done, Thumble Tumble started to rise into the air. It still felt like ground beneath her feet, but when she looked down it wasn't grass she was standing on anymore, it was seaweed. She fell to her knees with the force of the air pushing down against her as she rose fast into the sky. Whatever the creature was it didn't have four heads, only one. And she was standing right on top of it. She had walked backwards onto the loch and stepped right onto the head of the Ollpheist! The creature was soaring high in the sky. It had huge wings and a tail that had a point the shape of an arrowhead right at the tip.

There was seaweed draped over its head so she couldn't see what the hideous monster actually looked like. It circled once over the castle then flew straight at Rhino. Just before it reached him, there was a massive spray of water like the jet from twenty power hoses joined together. The force of the water lifted Rhino off his feet and smashed him against the castle gates. He banged his head on the huge iron gates then sank to the ground in a heap. The creature flew back up into the air and started a second circle around the castle. Rhino clambered to his feet and ran towards the hills.

Too late: the creature came at him from behind with another massive jet of water and this time the force pushed Rhino to the ground face first, then pushed his entire body twenty metres along the ground.

Rhino was sure next time it would be coming in for the kill. He mustered every bit of energy he could to get to his feet, then he ran as fast as he'd ever run in his entire life. He could barely catch a breath as he ran high into the hills, his chest pounding and the muscles in his legs burning. He didn't look back and he didn't stop until he was safely back in the hills where he finally drew breath and collapsed in a heap, relieved still to be alive.

Chapter 5

Let the games begin

MJ was busy preening himself as usual. He was the most arrogant of all Deer Folk and he had already spent hours combing his hair and polishing his antlers in preparation for the opening parade. He would be leading the gladiators into the arena and wanted to look his best – as always!

He was a champion of the games having won seven gold medals the previous year and lifting the Lazlo Cup for the ninth year in a row. He had already decided that this year would be number ten.

MJ was eight feet tall – ten if you included his antlers. He had long wavy blond hair and piercing green eyes. MJ was a very handsome beast and he knew it. When he trotted past the crowds of spectators he would wave his head from side to side so that his long hair would flow behind him, glistening in the sunlight.

There were ten games in total, although one game was a team sport, the tug o' war. MJ never took part in that game as he liked to stand out from the crowd and you can't do that in tug o' war! The tug o' war was very similar to the human version of the game with eight pullers – or 'tuggers' – per team pulling a giant rope in opposite directions. The winning team is the side that manages to pull the other side over the line in the middle of the two teams. The only difference is that in the Great Games they really take the war part of the game to heart. Each of the teams has another eight players, known as 'soldiers'. The soldiers fire arrows, cannon balls and boulders at the opposing team as they are pulling. If one of the pullers is hit then one of the soldiers can replace them as a substitute, and each team can have nine substitutes in total. All eight soldiers plus the coach can replace injured pullers.

The tug o' war was always the first of the games and it starts when the sun begins to set. There are eight teams competing at first, which results in four winners. The four teams then compete and the two winners of these games are in the final. The final is even more dangerous, as to add to the excitement the audience are given bags of darts to throw at the teams as they compete. The tug o' war has a lot of casualties, which is another reason why MJ never competed in it. He would not want to be hit on his beautiful face by a boulder or any other flying object lobbed into the arena.

There was a loud hale of trumpets and bagpipes sounding the competitors to take their places at the entrance of the arena. MJ was standing front and centre as the previous year's champion. The champion always leads the other competitors into the arena with their herd's flag held out in front. The Lochranza flag was purple with four squares. In three of the squares there was a picture. Top left a castle, top right a dragon's head, bottom left, an arrow and bottom right, blank. This is supposed to represent the invisible hypnotic gas that protects the castle, hence why there's nothing there!

MJ entered the arena with his head held high and the flag slightly off to the side. He didn't want the flag to block anyone's view of him! Immediately behind him were the Deer Folk of Lochranza, including one female competitor called Serena. MJ did not like Serena one bit. Not only was she a fantastic gladiator for a female, but she was also very beautiful with violet hair down to her waist and big wide eyes to match. MJ did not like anyone who was better looking than him.

There were twenty-five competitors from Lochranza. Behind them it was the Deer Folk from Skye, then Islay, Muck, Eigg, Rum, Canna and Tiree. In total, there were over two hundred gladiators competing for the Lazlo Cup.

Each gladiator bowed their head towards the royal box as they entered the arena behind MJ. King Rohan was standing tall in the box with Queen Sofia by his side. They both clapped every gladiator as they made their way into the arena. King Rohan was very handsome with a chisel jaw and dark hair which had patches of grey specks dotted randomly through it. Sofia was younger than Rohan. She had white hair and pale pink eyes like an albino. She was a gentle soul with a kind heart, which you could tell just from looking at her.

After circling the entire arena twice, MJ led the majority of the competitors to the side lines. The tug o' war teams headed to the centre of the arena and first up it was Islay versus Eigg. The contest was over in ten seconds with Islay the resounding victors. Not surprising, as the Deer Folk from Eigg are miniature and so only a few feet tall. Whereas the deer folk from Islay are tallest species of all Deer Folk, known as the big yins. The crowd erupted in an equal chorus of cheers and boos.

The tugs continued until the remaining two teams in the final were Muck and Rum. Funnily enough, both these teams resembled their island's names. The Deer Folk from Muck were filthy and the team from Rum were very tipsy from drinking large jugs of rum between every game. The games master shouted out "Tug!" and the two teams started to pull on their respective sides of the rope. Within a few seconds, three of the pullers on the Muck side had fallen. They had all been battered with the same huge boulder. Then, another two fell after being hit by darts from a group of older school kids standing in the front row of the arena. Five soldiers went on as substitutes. But, no sooner had they put their hands on the rope when there was another hail of darts from the row of kids and all five of them hit the deck. Bruiser was the coach of the Muck team. He was shouting from side line, "Get a grip, yah bunch of Jessies."

He was an enormous creature, easily fourteen feet tall with his huge antlers. His arms were as thick as tree trunks and he had a beard all the way down to his waist. He decided it was time for him to step in. He took hold of the rope, and with one fairly effortless tug, the entire Rum team went flying into the air and all fell on the other side of the line. They were hiccupping as they landed one on top of the other in a huge heap with hooves and antlers sticking out all over the place.

"And the winners are Muck!" hollered the games master as he walked over and took Bruiser's hand to raise it up in the air in victory. But, Bruiser was so tall that when the master of the games lifted his hand all the way above his head, Bruiser's arm only went up to shoulder level so it was more of a hand straight out in the air, victory punch. There was a huge roar of clapping all around the arena and then after about twenty seconds there was complete silence.

"Thank goodness that's over," grunted MJ. "Now we can get onto the more important events... the ones I'm in."

He strutted over to the archery. There was a row of very pretty cheerers each holding a large wooden bow in one hand and a quiver in the other. Each of the quivers had five long silver arrows sticking out. The cheerers passed the bows to the competitors and then started to dance. They kicked their front legs up high in the air, then spun around, shaking their brightly coloured pom-poms as they spun. Then they shook their short tails towards the spectators. They repeated this display several times singing as they danced, "Arrows go swift, do not drift, you have to be bold, if you plan to take gold."

The archers each took their places. First up was MJ, of course. He took aim. There was not so much as a whisper around the arena, then, *whoosh!* His silver arrow flew through the air and hit the target two hundred metres away, dead centre. There was a gushing around the arena as the female spectators burst into cheers.

Next up was Mac from Tiree. He was about the same height and build as MJ, but he had short red frizzy hair with a beard to match. He took aim and again hit the target dead centre.

The aim of the game of archery is that each contestant has five arrows and they must hit the target dead centre every time. But the target gets fifty metres further away with every shot.

By the time they got to the second last arrow the target was three hundred and fifty metres away and there were only four of the initial thirty gladiators left in the game, MJ, Mac, Serena and Geeza. Geeza was a bit of a ducker and a diver from the island of

Stornoway. Stornoway wasn't even competing in the games this year, but, Geeza had managed to acquire himself a place by using his great, great, great grandfather as his connection to the Isle of Canna. He was entered as a gladiator for Canna which caused some booing when he went up to shoot, as effectively he was cheating.

First to shoot was MJ, again. He aimed, he fired and hit the target dead centre again. The arena erupted. There were cheers and tears from those females who just couldn't take the excitement of seeing his tall, handsome body thrusting around the arena as he started a mini victory parade – even though the competition was still far from over! Next was Mac. He took aim, drew his bow all the way back and then let go. His silver arrow flew like a bolt of lightning towards the target but then landed just metres before it. The spectators clapped for such a gallant effort and Mac bowed his head to thank them for their support. He then trotted off to the side lines with the other archers who were now out of the competition.

Serena was next to take aim. She gently pulled back on the bow. So gently in fact, it looked as though the arrow would barely make it out of the bow let alone all the way to the target. The arrow glided from the bow, through the air and three hundred and fifty metres away hit the target right in the middle of the bull's-eye. Cheering erupted again around the arena. Next up stepped Geeza. The cheering was promptly replaced by booing. The crowd then fell silent as he pulled his great bow back. *Whoosh*, the arrow went hurtling through the air at the speed of light and hit the target, just off centre. He was out. The crowd did not boo. Instead, this time they clapped their hands and Geeza bowed his head in thanks and walked off to join the other archers.

It was now the last arrow each and the target was placed four hundred metres away. MJ took aim as he had every other time. He let the last silver arrow go and bang, it hit the target right in the centre. He turned and grinned at Serena, then murmured, "Beat that if you can."

Serena moved to the marker, took aim and just as she did MJ muttered under his breath, so that only Serena could hear, "Make sure you don't break a nail."

Serena didn't even turn to look at him. She focused on the target, and then just as before gently pulled back on her bow. The arrow flew gracefully through the air as if floating on an invisible cushion but instead of aiming for her own target, the arrow was heading for MJ's. Next thing the crowd started stamping their hooves and shouting, "Winner, winner, winner!" Serena's arrow had split straight through MJ's arrow, breaking it in two and causing it to fall to the ground. Only one arrow remained in the target: Serena's.

MJ took the bow off his back and threw it to the ground. When the spectators clapped him, instead of bowing in thanks he turned and trotted off into the changing rooms under the stadium without so much as even congratulating Serena as he went.

Serena gracefully bowed her head to the cheering spectators, then again to receive her gold medal from the games master. There are no silver or bronze medals awarded at the games. There is only one winner per game and they receive the gold medal. The gladiator with the most gold medals at the end of the games wins the Lazlo Cup. The only game that isn't included is the team game, the tug o' war. There was a separate medal awarded to the coach of the winning team, which he could pass to the best member of his team if he wanted, and that would count as one gold medal for that gladiator.

The score after the first two games was zero medals for MJ!

Chapter 6

The Secret of the Ollpheist

When the creature was sure Rhino had gone it flew back down towards Lochranza Castle and landed gently beside the huge iron gates. It lay its head flat on the ground and Thumble Tumble sat down then slid to the ground, just as if coming down off of a big slide. The creature's huge head then rose back up and started to shake side to side. As it did, large chunks of seaweed flew off landing all around Thumble Tumble's feet. The creature was roaring as its head waved from side to side.

At first, Thumble Tumble thought the creature was hollering in pain, then she realised it sounded more like laughter. She looked up to see the hideous monster's head, but instead of twenty peering spider's eyes and a set of poisonous pincers there was a dragon with a huge smile laughing back at her. With all the seaweed now scattered over the grass, parts of the castle wall and the gates, Thumble Tumble could see that the Ollpheist wasn't a four headed scary monster. But a giant purple dragon, with big round green eyes, and a green tip at the end of its long purple tail.

"That was such a laugh," said the creature.

Thumble Tumble took a step back in shock as she didn't know dragons could speak. The creature leaned down and put his arm out and wrapped it around her back. Thumble Tumble jumped with fright, but when the creature just kept smiling at her she realised he had only put his arm out to stop her from tripping over the large chunks of seaweed lying on the ground around her feet. "Who, who are you?" she said trembling.

"Please don't be afraid," said the creature. "I was only trying to help you. I'm Jock, the last of the Sea Dragons."

Thumble Tumble had never heard of a Sea Dragon before. Without thinking, she blurted out, "And what makes a Sea Dragon different from an ordinary dragon?"

When she realised how rude she sounded she apologised and asked simply, "What's a Sea Dragon?"

"Well," said Jock. "Instead of breathing fire, we breathe water, lots of water. During the great battle, when the coven was broken we helped the white witches fight evil. As the water we breathe is so pure it can actually melt a dark witch if she is blasted with it for long enough. Usually thirty seconds does the trick but for a particularly evil witch it can take twice as long."

Wow, thought Thumble Tumble. "It must be amazing to have the power to melt a dark witch."

Jock's eyes glazed over and he looked as though he was about to burst into tears. "It is pretty cool," he said, "but also sad because every Sea Dragon on earth was destroyed by the dark witches except me. When they found out about our special powers, Mogdred, the supreme dark witch, ordered the destruction of all Sea Dragons. It was just over eight years ago when the last of the Sea Dragons were slain. They were my parents. I was still an egg and just before the dark witches came my parents took me to Domhain Loch. They tied a large rock to my shell and dropped me into the loch to try to protect me. When I hatched, I was so small I didn't know what to do and so I swam straight to the surface, where fortunately I was seen by King Rohan.

"He nurtured me along with the help of his beautiful wife, Queen Sofia. If it hadn't been for them I would never have survived. They gave me food and they also started the rumour of the Ollpheist. The terrible four-headed monster that lives at the bottom of Domhain Loch. They did it to stop any creatures coming near the loch. They even made up stories of Deer Folk going into the loch looking for the monster and then disappearing. Before long the rumours became reality and I became legend, the legend of the Ollpheist.

"I have had to hide in the loch my entire life, as if any dark witches found out that there was still a Sea Dragon alive they would hunt me down and kill me. To be honest, it's pretty lonely being the last Sea Dragon on earth."

Thumble Tumble had a lump in her throat. She too had lost her parents when she was very young. So young, in fact, that she couldn't remember them at all. But at least she had her aunts and she couldn't even begin to imagine how lonely it must be for Jock with no family, all alone at the bottom of the loch.

Jock waded into the loch and rested his head on the shore and Thumble Tumble sat down beside him. She told Jock all about her Auntie Bessie's wacky spells and Auntie Isla's Scoffalicious Chocolate that she was delivering to King Rohan so she could sneak into the great games. She took off her pink converse trainers and dipped her feet in the water as they spoke. She was still wearing her stripy tights! The water was icy cold and it sent a tingling feeling up through her legs that felt fab. Thumble Tumble had wanted to put her feet in Domhain Loch for a long time, but she had been too afraid to do it in case her toes were eaten by the Ollpheist!

"Not much chance of that," said Jock. "I'm a vegetarian. I mainly eat seaweed and the occasional giant of course," he said jokingly. They both burst out laughing.

They were having so much fun they hadn't noticed that the sky above them had gone almost completely black and that the air had started to turn very chilly.

Chapter 7

Spoil sports

MJ was still in the changing rooms grunting and moaning at the fact he'd been beaten by a girl, and a beautiful girl at that. *Could things get any worse?* he thought. Then, from above the changing rooms, he could hear what sounded like a stampede of hooves followed by very loud screaming. Not the kind of screaming he was used to. It wasn't the sound of girls screaming fanatically, but actual screams of fear.

MJ bolted back up to the arena as fast as he could. There were Deer Folk running in all directions. The competitors were running towards the stands away from the arena whilst the spectators were running onto the arena away from the stands. They were crashing into each other with their antlers getting tangled and stuck making them fall to the ground. Then amongst all the chaos MJ heard a whooshing sound go straight past his left ear. It felt red hot, as though his ear had been grazed by fire. Next there was a loud crashing sound beside his left hoof and he looked down to see the ground cracked open where a thunderbolt had struck the ground leaving a black powder circle to mark the spot. When he looked up, he knew instantly they were under attack from Night Witches. But how had they gotten in past the tower guards?

There were dozens of magic bolts raining down on them from the black skies above. They had to take cover. MJ headed straight for the centre of the arena and the hail of thunder bolts followed him taking their aim away from the panicked crowds of spectators. MJ flicked his long blond hair to attract even more attention and sure enough more thunderbolts headed his way.

He shouted to the cheerers who had run to the side lines, "Get the school kids and take cover in the changing rooms."

The cheerers immediately followed his royal highness's instructions. MJ was King Rohan's son, Prince of Lochranza. He was extremely agile and moved swiftly from side to side dodging the thunder bolts as he led them further away from the spectators into the centre of the arena.

Although he was extremely arrogant, MJ was also very brave and would do anything to protect his people from harm. "Where are my parents?" he called to the royal guards.

Before they could answer, MJ saw the king and queen leading the fleeing spectators into the castle. King Rohan was fiercely fighting off Night Witches alongside his guards and Queen Sofia was helping to carry the injured inside.

MJ was soon joined in the arena by Mac and Geeza. They both had their bows in hand and quivers stoked full of arrows slung over their backs. Geeza was carrying a spare bow which he threw over to MJ. Then, from out of nowhere appeared Serena with MJ's quiver also jammed full of arrows.

The four gladiators started to shoot huge silver arrows into the air towards the black Night Witches circling above their heads. The witches were circling so fast it was difficult to hit them. They were hard to spot, as they stayed within the dark clouds making them virtually invisible. Mac took aim and hit the back of a broom. The broom started spinning out of control and threw the witch off, far into the Giant Hills beside the castle. MJ managed to shoot straight through one of the black brooms. But as the witch was falling to the ground, another zoomed in and grabbed her then shot off back into the clouds.

Mac hit another Night Witch, then Geeza got one, and then MJ. Four were now spinning frantically out of control on their brooms. Surprisingly, Serena hadn't manage to hit a single Night Witch, having been such an excellent shot in the archery competition. The four gladiators stood back to back to form a small square in the centre of the arena and fired their arrows miles up into the dark clouds, forcing the Night Witches back, away from the fleeing spectators. The Night Witches came back at them in force, firing dozens of bolts from all directions. The bolts kept blasting at them, fast and furious. The Night Witches formed a circle above the gladiators' heads and then started swooping towards them in pairs, firing lightning bolts with every swoop. Mac fell to the ground. He had been hit on the shoulder and blood was pouring onto the arena floor. "Cover Mac," MJ shouted to Serena.

As he turned to fire his next arrow, a bolt went hurtling past his head towards Mac's injured body. MJ tried to grab the bolt with his hand, but he was too slow. The lightning bolt passed straight through his fingers, singeing the tips and hit Mac. This time the bolt struck him on his leg just above the knee. Night Witches surrounded them and they were closing in. MJ knew it was only a matter of time before they ran out of arrows, and then they would be sitting ducks.

Mac was now bleeding heavily and needed help soon, or he could die.

MJ grabbed Mac's good arm. "You'll have to run on three legs, can you manage it?"

Mac nodded.

"OK, on the count of three we go. "One, two—"

Before he could say *three* another lightning bolt crashed down and sent MJ, Geeza and Serena hurtling to the ground.

MJ jumped back up, as quick as a flash and grabbed three arrows from his bow. He fired the arrows simultaneously at the three Night Witches who were heading towards them. Each had a death bolt in their hand, aimed straight at the fallen gladiators. MJ hit all three of the witches who shrieked and wailed as they fell to the ground. He was still loading his bow when two more witches appeared.

"Get him out of here!" MJ pointed at Mac as he shouted to Serena and Geeza. But, instead of helping to pick up Mac, Serena took a arrow from her quiver and stabbed Geeza in the back with it. Geeza fell beside Mac. He looked as though he was dead. His body lay completely still and his eyes were wide open staring up into the dark skies above.

MJ couldn't believe what was happening. Serena was helping the Night Witches and now two of his friends were lying dead or dying. MJ charged at the oncoming Night Witches. He was like a raging bull going for red with his head bowed low and his long piercing antlers out in front of him. Just as he did, Serena lifted her bow and took aim.

Chapter 8

Melting Pot

Thumble Tumble suddenly had a feeling of dread coming over her. She had felt this type of cold before, when she was a little girl. This wasn't a normal rush of cold air. The air was icy cold and cut right into her bones. It felt like someone was holding ice cold needles and poking them into her skin. And the darkness was not the dark of night. It was as though someone had lifted a giant dark grey blanket and placed it over the sky. There was not a slither of light to be seen. No stars or moons in the distance, just a huge black cloud that went on forever.

Then, almost as quickly as it had arrived, the chilling darkness started to disappear. The air got slightly warmer and Thumble Tumble could feel the tips of her fingers again. They were tingling as though she had just plunged them into boiling hot water. When she looked up to the sky, there were scores of light starting to cut through the black clouds. "Thank goodness they've gone. I think that was the Night Witches, Jock. They must have seen you, or that horrible giant told them about you."

Jock was still looking up at the sky when he replied, "I don't think they're looking for me."

Thumble Tumble looked back up and saw the most gigantic cyclone of black and grey clouds forming right above Lochranza Castle. In amongst the clouds she could see the very vague outline of what looked like witches on brooms flying into the cyclone towards the castle.

"Come on, we have to help them!" cried Thumble Tumble as she sprung to her feet and started running towards her broom.

Jock didn't move a muscle. He was frozen to the spot.

"I'm sorry, Thumble Tumble," he said in a trembling voice. "I can't come with you. If they see me they'll know there's still a living Sea Dragon and they'll hunt me down until I'm dead."

Thumble Tumble could see the fear in Jock's eyes. She didn't want to put him in danger, so without uttering another word she just hopped onto her broom, and headed for the castle.

Thumble Tumble flew straight into the castle without a single arrow trying to stop her. There were no Deer Folk guarding the perimeter from the turrets. This was really strange, so she looked back to see what had happened to the guards in the turrets, when suddenly, she hit into something and went flying off her broom. Luckily she wasn't that far off the ground and so didn't have too far to fall. When she landed she realised she had banged into a beautiful female Deer Folk, with long violet hair, which was now twisted around Thumble Tumble's waist.

"I'm so sorry," Thumble Tumble said as she started to untangle the long strands of hair.

"Don't make another move," said MJ as he stood over Thumble Tumble with a huge silver arrow aimed straight at her chest.

Thumble Tumble looked down shaking and saw that the arrow wasn't pointed at her chest, but at Serena's hand as it held a dagger poised to stab Thumble Tumble right in the heart.

Serena dropped the dagger, and Thumble Tumble finished detaching herself from her hair as fast as she could.

"Who are you?" asked MJ, as he started to tie Serena's hands behind her back.

"I'm Thumble Tumble. I was supposed to be delivering Scoffalicious Chocolate to King Rohan for my Auntie Isla."

MJ stopped in his tracks. He took a long look at Thumble Tumble then said, "So you're Lizzie's daughter? We'd better get you out of here. Pronto!"

"Can you help me with these two?" he said.

"No problem," replied Thumble Tumble, and she leaned down to help Mac onto his hooves.

She then placed her broom under his arm like a crutch. MJ was still leaning over Geeza's lifeless body, when without warning Geeza bolted upright into a sitting position, and with his bow in his hand he fired. The shot took out the most hideous Night Witch flying directly towards them.

"You guys run. I'll give you cover!" he shouted as he pulled another arrow from his quiver.

"I'm not leaving you," hollered MJ.

"I won't make it, the wound is too deep."

"Try," pleaded MJ.

"I can't stand up. Please, you need to save the others," said Geeza.

MJ turned around just in time to see another dozen Night Witches swooping towards them in a death circle. There were no arrows left in his quiver. He took his bow and swung it around his head then let go. The bow swung past all twelve witches knocking them to the ground one at a time. Then it came back round like a boomerang straight into his hand. Just as he caught the bow a lightning bolt hit his hand blasting the bow right out of it. The bow landed on the ground twenty feet away. They were surrounded.

The Night Witches were circling above their heads, faster and faster, cackling with glee. They each pointed a long black finger towards their target and started to chant the death bolt spell, then, *blast!*

Before the death bolts could be summoned, a huge jet of water blasted the circle of witches apart. They started to fizzle and fry as the pure water poured down on them. Their brooms completely disintegrated as soon as the water touched them and then a few seconds later the witches themselves started to melt. There was black smoke bellowing from the witches' cloaks as they started melting. The smoke was so thick that neither MJ nor Thumble Tumble could see a thing.

Jock flew towards them. "Run!" he shouted, then he flew back up into the air and fired another huge jet of water into the circle of Night Witches.

Thumble Tumble grabbed Geeza under his arms and started dragging him towards the castle. Mac was hobbling alongside still using Thumble Tumble's broom as a crutch. They could hear the Night Witches flying away, back up into the black cyclone they had arrived in.

When the smoke cleared, all that remained of the Night Witches were a few charred cloaks lying like puddles on the ground and some grey ash where their brooms had disintegrated. There was no sign of Serena, or any explanation as to why she had helped the Night Witches attack them.

Chapter 9

Lazlo's Cup

Thumble Tumble let go of Geeza's arm as soon as they entered the great hall inside the castle. Right away two of the cheerers were by his side. One had a long sharp needle with steel thread and the other had her arms full of bandages. They set to work straight away stitching up the huge gash in Geeza's side, then wrapping him up in so many bandages he looked like a mummy.

Mac was also being looked after by two equally beautiful cheerers who were tending to his leg and shoulder wounds.

"Here you go, miss," he said to Thumble Tumble, handing her broom back. "We are forever in your debt. If you hadn't arrived when you did the Night Witches would have killed us for sure." Mac had a deep, pounding voice.

Thumble Tumble felt as though she recognised his voice, as though she had met Mac before. In fact she was sure she had met all of them before – Mac, MJ and Geeza.

"This is Lizzie's daughter," MJ announced.

"I might have known," said Mac. "No ordinary girl would try to take on a group of Night Witches armed with just a broom!"

"Did you know my mother?" asked Thumble Tumble.

"That we did, young lady. A finer witch I've never met. We fought together to protect the coven from the Night Witches and she put her life on the line many times to save others."

He was just about to launch into a full speech when King Rohan entered the hall.

"I think that's enough chat of the past," he said glaring towards Mac.

"I'd really like to know more about my mother. I didn't even know she had fought against the Night Witches."

"I'm afraid that's a conversation for another day," said the King. "Anyway, we still have eight magnificent games to watch and I was wondering if you and Jock would care to join us in the Royal Box?"

"Would we ever," replied Thumble Tumble excitedly. They followed the King through the great hall to a narrow staircase that spiralled up to the top level of the castle walls. Although it was a bit tight, Jock was determined not to miss this great opportunity, so he squeezed himself up the stairs and through an opening at the top, no bigger than a standard door entrance. When he popped through the entrance he found himself in the Royal Box. It was enormous and certainly not what he'd expected as he'd squashed his huge body between the stair rails the whole way up. There were no seats in the box, just a small bench along the viewing deck. It was a very plush bench, with gold legs and the cushion was covered in a deep purple velvet material. This was not for sitting on. It was so that the King and Queen could kneel down on their front legs if they got tired.

Queen Sofia was already in the box when they entered along with two royal guards and a strange looking little man with a big red whistle and lots of bits of paper. Thumble Tumble bowed as soon as she saw the Queen and Jock bent over as much as he could. Not quite a bow, but as close as he could get to one with his huge stomach. "Please stand up, my dear," said the Queen in the softest most comforting voice. "This is our games master, Mr Pimbleton." She pointed to the strange little man.

"Well I'd better get back to the arena," said Mr Pimbleton.

He nodded at Thumble Tumble and Jock as he left the Royal Box. No sooner had he walked through the doorway when he was standing right in the middle of the arena below, blowing his big red whistle.

Everything had settled down. The gladiators were back on the field and the spectators were back in their viewing boxes. The cheerers had cleared up the remains of the Night Witches and the entire arena was now lit by giant burning torches that were situated all along the top of the castle walls as night had fallen.

There were three gladiators missing from the games, Serena, Geeza and MJ. MJ had decided not to participate further this year, and instead joined his young guest alongside his parents and Jock in the Royal Box. Mac had been bandaged up and was back in the arena with his two beautiful cheerers looking after him.

The next of the games was 'Throwing the Boulder'. As the name suggests the aim of the game is to throw a boulder. Each contestant has one throw. They have to select a boulder and throw it as far as they can. The winner is the one who throws the heaviest boulder the furthest. The only slight catch to the game is that the gladiators are blind folded and have to use their instincts so as not to throw any boulders at the spectators.

This had not always proven to be a good idea, and in the past many spectators had ended up with boulders flying towards them during the game.

"This is why the Royal Box is so high up," laughed Queen Sofia.

The competition was well under way, with most of the gladiators having thrown already. Two of the gladiators from Rum threw their boulders straight into the spectators on the south wall, injuring more Deer Folk with their poor aim than the Night Witches had managed to do during their attack!

There were five gladiators left to throw. Just as the next gladiator lifted his massive boulder above his head, two witches came flying into the arena in a vale of purple smoke. The guards in the Royal Box quickly took aim and drew their bows to fire into the ball of smoke.

"Stillamomentum," said Auntie Bessie.

Everyone stood motionless, except Auntie Isla and Auntie Bessie. They flew into the royal box and dismounted from their brooms. Within a few seconds the effects of the 'pausing spell' wore off. The poor gladiator who had been holding the massive boulder above his head couldn't hold the weight any longer, and it dropped right onto his two front hooves.

"We are so sorry to interrupt, Your Majesties, but we were extremely worried about Thumble Tumble. We had told her to be home before dark!"

Auntie Isla was now glaring towards Thumble Tumble, waiting for an explanation.

"Please don't be angry, Isla," said Queen Sofia. "If it wasn't for Thumble Tumble we would have lost some of our finest gladiators to the Night Witches". Queen Sofia told Isla and Bessie about the day's events, and how brave Thumble Tumble had been in the fight against the Night Witches.

Thumble Tumble was surprised by how well her aunties seemed to know the Queen. They spoke as though they were old friends. But Thumble Tumble had never heard them speak about the Queen before. The Queen invited Isla and Bessie to join them for the remainder of the games and the three of them chatted quietly at the back of the box.

Thumble Tumble tried to overhear what they were talking about but the cheers from the spectators were too loud, and she was enjoying the games so much she soon forgot they were there.

The games continued well into the night and it was past midnight when the last game finished and the champion of the gladiators was announced. Mr Pimbleton was standing in the centre of the arena with a little rusty cup. He had swapped his red whistle for a bright yellow megaphone which he was now tapping frantically to test the volume.

"Ladies and gentlemen, with a total of six medals the winner of the Lazlo Cup this year is Mac of Tiree."

There was a huge uproar around the arena and the spectators started clapping and stamping their hooves in celebration.

The rusty little cup didn't look very grand. In fact it didn't look like the proper cup for such a prestigious competition. Looks however can be deceiving, and this little cup held a great power, the power to melt a frozen heart. The cup had been enchanted thousands of years earlier by a powerful wizard called Lazlo. He had fallen in love with a beautiful princess called Jacqueline Frost – sister of Jack. But her heart was made of ice so cold that she couldn't love him back. Lazlo was distraught, so he travelled to the Earth's core and forged a cup made from the molten iron ore found at the centre of the earth. He then cast a magical spell that transfers the power of the smouldering heat into the person drinking from the cup. When Jacqueline drank from the cup her ice cold heart melted and she fell in love with Lazlo. She could never go back to the icy cold land where she had lived with her brother Jack. So from that day on, it was only 'Jack Frost' who would go out to play on a frosty day.

The story of Lazlo and Jacqueline made the gladiators think that the cup had the power to make someone fall in love with them. They fought fiercely each year to win the cup and gain true love. Unfortunately, it was only after they won that they would find out the cup didn't have the power to make someone fall in love. It only had the power to melt an ice-cold heart!

Mac walked over to the winner's podium, but instead of taking the cup he whispered something into Mr Pimbleton's ear. A second later Mr Pimbleton had disappeared from the arena and was now standing right beside Thumble Tumble in the Royal Box. "I'm afraid we need you at the podium, my dear." As he spoke he took hold of Thumble

Tumble's hand and in the blink of an eye she was standing beside Mac on the winner's podium.

Mr Pimbleton then got his bright yellow megaphone and announced, "Ladies and gentlemen, in a surprise turn of events, the winner of the Lazlo Cup this year is Thumble Tumble. The cup has been given to her by Mac for her bravery, excellent battle skills, but mainly for saving his life!"

Mr Pimbleton had a little chuckle. He then handed Thumble Tumble the little rusty cup and shook her hand so much she thought her arm was going to pop out of its socket.

Thumble Tumble held the cup high in the air and the whole arena erupted in loud cheering. She had thought the games would be awesome, but they were way better than she had imagined. She just couldn't picture the day getting any better, until Auntie Isla announced that the Scoffalicious Chocolate was now ready to eat. Thumble Tumble and Jock took a huge chunk each and sat back as they watched the cheerers performing their dances again until well into the wee hours, when they both headed home, stuffed, exhausted and best friends.

Chapter 10

Return of the Protector

Serena opened her eyes slowly. She couldn't see a thing, the room was in complete darkness. It was ice cold and the air was thick with the most putrid stench, like rotten cabbages. The smell almost made her sick. She put her hands out to feel her surroundings. She felt what she thought must be a wall. It was cold and slimy with some kind of gooey liquid dripping from it down onto the floor below. She felt her way all around the room. There were no doors or windows and not a solitary ray of light anywhere.

She couldn't quite remember how she had got here, but she knew exactly where she was. In Mogdred's dungeon. The last thing she could remember was being pulled up into the air and then being hit by a thunderous bolt. The force of the bolt was piercing and painful and so strong that it knocked her out.

She was still dazed when she heard a familiar voice from the corner of the room. "You failed us. I held up my part of the bargain – you were winning. But you couldn't even defeat a child and her pet dragon!"

There was a dull light now moving across the room towards her. Mogdred was pointing her long black finger straight at Serena's head. She hissed as she spoke and her horrible breath made Serena want to throw up even more.

"The dragon certainly defeated your army," Serena barked back at Mogdred.

She was fearless, even with the most evil of all of the Night Witches standing over her about to cast a death spell.

"Don't worry, Serena," said Mogdred in a low eerie voice. "We will hunt the Sea Dragon down. We killed every other Sea Dragon on the planet so I'm sure we'll manage one more."

Mogdred started cackling at the thought of killing Jock, the very last of the Sea Dragons.

She drew in a long deep breath and then started to chant a death spell.

Serena interrupted her. "Anyway, it's the child you should be seeking, not the dragon".

Mogdred kept chanting. "Death shall not be swift, death shall be painful". Serena felt as if there was a huge invisible hand around her throat getting tighter and tighter, choking every last drop of life from her body. She couldn't breathe and was just about to pass out when she managed to utter a few words.

Mogdred released her spell immediately. "What did you say?" She shrieked at Serena who was now rolling around on the floor, gasping for breath.

"She has the power of the protector."

"How do you know this?" Mogdred was now standing over Serena glaring at her with her white eyes wide open.

Serena noticed for the first time that Mogdred had no eyelids. *This must be why she had to stay in the dungeons of her own castle,* thought Serena. *Any light at all must cause her excruciating pain.*

She was still staring into Mogdred's eyes when Mogdred grabbed her by her forearms and hauled her up onto her four legs. "I asked you a question. If you answer correctly you may just live."

Serena took a moment and then said, "She wears the ring. A pink tear drop made from glass."

Many stories of the protector's powers had been told over the years since Lizzie's death. But the one story that held true was that the power of the protector had been transferred to a baby via an amulet. The amulet was a small, pink glass ring, just like the one Serena had seen on Thumble Tumble's little finger.

"Well done, Serena. You live to fight another day... for me." Mogdred was almost grinning, although it was difficult to see any kind of emotion in her expressionless face.

"We had a deal," said Serena, gritting her teeth with anger.

"Yes, and now we have another deal. Your life in exchange for your services. I am going to need someone to track down this little witch and her dragon so that I can destroy them."

"Is it agreed, or will I continue my death spell where I left off?"

Serena bowed in agreement and once again she felt the piercing pain of a thunderbolt straight into her chest. When she lifted her head again she was standing at the bottom of a quiet road, with five little white cottages dotted along it and a cemetery at the top.